D1505196

■ この絵本の楽しみかた

● 日本文と英文のいずれでも物語を楽しめます。

● 英文は和文に基づいて詩のように書かれています。巻末Notes
　を参考にして素晴らしい英詩文を楽しんでください。

● この「日本昔ばなし」の絵はかっての人気絵本「講談社の絵本」
　全203巻の中から厳選されたものです。

■ **About this book**

● The story is bilingual, written in both English and Japanese.

● The English is not a direct translation of the Japanese, but
  rather a retelling of the same story in verse form. Enjoy
  the English on its own, using the helpful Notes at the back.

● The illustrations are selected from volume 203 of the
  Kodansha no ehon (Kodansha Picture Books) series.

Distributed in the United States by Kodansha America, Inc., and
in the United Kingdom and continental Europe by Kodansha
Europe Ltd.

Published by Kodansha International Ltd., 17-14 Otowa 1-chome,
Bunkyo-ku, Tokyo 112-8652, and Kodansha America. Inc.

First edition, 1993
Small-format edition, 1996
12 11 10 09 08 07 06 05   15 14 13 12 11 10 9

www.kodansha-intl.com

和 英 併記

日本昔ばなし

いっすんぼうし

THE INCH-HIGH SAMURAI

え●かさまつ しろう

Illustrations by **Shiro Kasamatsu**
Retold by **Ralph F. McCarthy**

KODANSHA INTERNATIONAL
Tokyo · New York · London

In Ná025niwa, in old Japan,
There lived a woman and a man
Who hadn't any children,
    so they spent their days alone

むかしむかしの　おはなしです。
おおさかに　すむ，　こだからに　めぐまれない
　　　　　ふうふが，　すみよしたいしゃに
こどもを　さずけて　くださいと　いのりました。

4

But every evening, rain or shine,
They'd go to Sumiyoshi Shrine
And pray for just one tiny little
baby of their own.

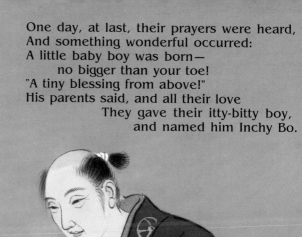

One day, at last, their prayers were heard,
And something wonderful occurred:
A little baby boy was born—
　　no bigger than your toe!
"A tiny blessing from above!"
His parents said, and all their love
　　　　They gave their itty-bitty boy,
　　　　　and named him Inchy Bo.

やがて　ねがいは　かないましたが,
さずけられた　こどもは
てのひらに　のる　ほどの
ちいさな　こどもでした。　それでも
ふたりは　おおよろこびで
いっすんぼうしと　なづけました。

He never did get very tall
(In fact, he didn't grow at all),
But Inchy never let that hold him back
    or get him down.
He was a cheerful, healthy lad
Who always helped his mum and dad,
And swore one day he'd be
    a samurai of great renown.

ちいさい　からだに　おおきな　ゆめを　もった
いっすんぼうしは，　りっぱな　ぶしに　なろうと
こころに　きめて　いました。

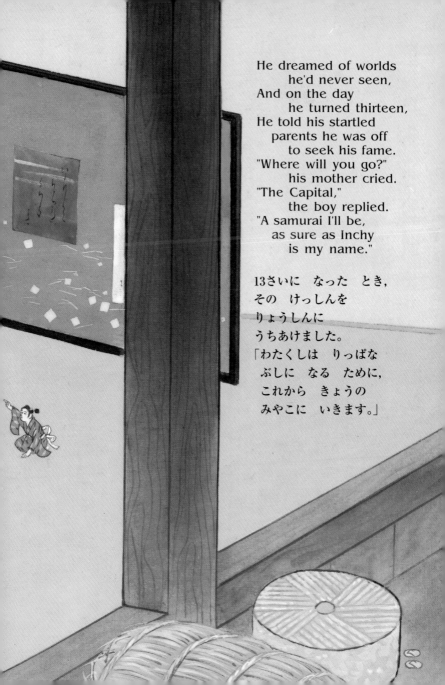

He dreamed of worlds
      he'd never seen,
And on the day
      he turned thirteen,
He told his startled
   parents he was off
      to seek his fame.
"Where will you go?"
      his mother cried.
"The Capital,"
      the boy replied.
"A samurai I'll be,
   as sure as Inchy
      is my name."

13さいに　なった　とき,
その　けっしんを
りょうしんに
うちあけました。
「わたくしは　りっぱな
　ぶしに　なる　ために,
　これから　きょうの
　みやこに　いきます。」

His father said:
"You'll need a boat
To get that far.
This ought to float,"
And gave the boy
a rice bowl,
with a chopstick
for an oar.

Mum's needle m[...]
a perfect swor[...]
She also put so[...]
food aboard—
An ear of rice
(enough to last
her son a wee[...]
or more).

いっすんぼうしは
おかあさんから
はりを　もらって
かたなに　し，
おとうさんからは
ふねに　する　おわんと
かいに　する　はしを
もらいました。

13

Down to the riverbank they went,
And there the kindly couple sent
Their Inchy out into the world
    and prayed he'd be okay.
"Goodbye, Dad! Take good care of Mum
I shall return, once I've become
A big, important man!"
    he shouted as he rowed away.

「おとうさん，　おかあさん，　いって　まいります。」
いっすんぼうしは　きょうを　めざします。
どこからともなく　うたが　ながれて　きました。
　　　おわんの　ふねに　はしの　かい
　　　きょうへ　はるばる　のぼりゆく

きょうへの　たびは　ながく
きけんな　ものでした。
それでも　いっすんぼうしは
ゆうきを　だして
きけんを　のりきりました。

16

It was a long and risky trip—
For days he rowed his rice-bowl ship
Against the current with his heavy,
    wooden chopstick oar.
And once, caught in a thunderstorm,
All soaking wet, and far from warm,
He nearly sank beneath the waves
    before he reached the shore.

Young Inchy knew he'd finally neared
The Capital, when lights appeared—
The river was much wider here,
    and boats were everywhere.
That night he rested in the reeds
And dreamed of doing valiant deeds,
And all night long the moon
    watched over him with loving care

みずぎわの　あしの　なかで　ねる　ことも　ありました。
みる　ゆめは　いつも　りっぱな　ぶしに　なって
りょうしんに　よろこんで　もらう　ゆめでした。

19

とうとう，きょうの みやこに つきました。
ごじょうの はしの らんかんに のぼって
みわたす きよみずの おてらも
かもがわの うつくしい ながれも
はじめて みる すばらしい けしきでした。

At last he reached the Capital.
So big! So bright! So magical!
As beautiful as anything
     he ever dreamed he'd see.
He climbed the rail of Gojo Bridge
To view the river, and the ridge
Where Kiyomizu Temple lay,
     in all its majesty.

Downtown,
all sorts
of passersby,
From flower girls
to samurai,
Went to and fro
where shops
sold everything
beneath
the sun.
Our Inchy dodged
between
their feet
And walked
about from
street to street,
Until he reached
the edge of town
when day was
nearly done.

いっすんぼうしは　きょうの　まちを
けんぶつして　まわりました。

さんじょうの　だいじんの　ごてんの　まえに
たった　いっすんぼうしは，
おおごえで　いいました。
「ごめんください，　ごめんください。」
「さて，　こえが　したようだが，　すがたが　みえぬ。」
と，　さんじょうの　だいじんは　さがします。
「ここです。
　わたくしは　あしだの　ところに　います。」
いっすんぼうしは　おおごえで　こたえました。

And there he saw a huge estate.
He boldly strode inside the gate
And wandered through the garden,
     stopping at the mansion stair.
He stood and shouted, loud and clear:
"Hello! Is anybody here?"
The Lord of Sanjo stepped outside and said:
     "What's that? Who's there?"

"Down here!" cried Inchy. "Look! It's me!"
His Lordship was amazed to see
This bean-sized boy. "How now!" said he,
    and placed him on his fan.
"My name is Inchy Bo, and I
Would like to be a samurai."
"I'll hire you then," the lord replied,
    "you charming little man."

「おまえは　いったい，　なにものだ。」
「いっすんぼうしと　もうします。
　どうぞ　けらいに　して　ください。」
と　たのみました。
さんじょうのだいじんは　いっすんぼうしを
むすめの　はるひめの　ごえいに　とりたてました。
いっすんぼうしは　はるひめに
いっしょうけんめい　つかえました。

あるひのことです。はるひめのかいた
たんざくが　かぜに　ふかれて
さくらの　こえだに　ひっかかると，
いっすんぼうしは　こえだを　つたって，
たんざくを　とりあげました。

His Lordship asked the boy to be
A guard for Lady Haru. She
Was just his age, and beautiful—
the great man's only daughter.
"So cute!" she said. "And yet, so brave!"
When Inchy risked his life to save
A cherry-blossom poem she'd made,
from falling in the water.

おおきな　のぞみを　もつ
いっすんぼうしには、
はるひめも　こころを
ひかれました。
はるひめは　いっすんぼうしの
ちいさい　ことを
たいそう　ざんねんがりました。

The two were never far apart,
And Inchy won the lady's heart
As time went by. Sometimes she'd sigh:
　　"If only he were taller!"
Each evening they would sit and read;
He learned with such amazing speed
That people called him "Inchy Bo,
　　the bodyguard and scholar."

ある はれた ひの ことです。
はるひめは いっすんぼうしと おともを つれて，
きよみずの おてらへ おまいりに いきました。

One day in spring, the lady and
Her maids and bodyguards had planned
To visit Kiyomizu Temple—
        Inchy led the way.
They saw the cherry-blossoms there,
And had their lunch, and said a prayer,
But as they gaily headed homeward
        later in the day . . .

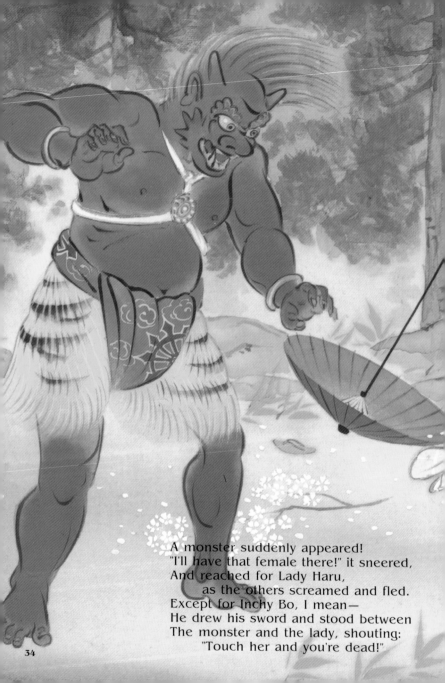

A monster suddenly appeared!
"I'll have that female there!" it sneered,
And reached for Lady Haru,
    as the others screamed and fled.
Except for Inchy Bo, I mean—
He drew his sword and stood between
The monster and the lady, shouting:
    "Touch her and you're dead!"

34

その　かえりみち,
おおきな　あかおにが　あらわれて,
おそいかかりました。　おともの　ものは,
われさきにと　にげだして　しまいました。
のこったのは　いっすんぼうしだけです。
「ぶれいもの。　さがれ！」
いっすんぼうしは　あかおにを
にらみつけました。

35

"Yum, yum! A snack!" the monster roared
And swallowed Inchy (and his sword).
Now Haru would be eaten, too!
    At least, that's how it seemed—

ところが　あかおには
いっすんぼうしを　つまみあげ，
ぱくっと　のみこんで
しまいました。　おなかに　はいった
いっすんぼうしは　はりの　かたなを　ぬくと
あたりかまわず　つきさしましたから，
あかおには　たまりません。

But Inchy, in the belly of
The beast, kept fighting for his love:
He poked about inside it, till it
　　danced and howled and screamed.

So badly was the monster hurt,
It spit the boy out in the dirt
And ran off crying bitter tears,
    and never did return.
"My hero!" Lady Haru cried.
"Without you I'd have surely died!"
"Are you all right?" said Inchy.
    "That's my only real concern."

「いたい　いたい，　これは　かなわん。」
あかおには　いっすんぼうしを
はきだすと，　にげて　いきました。
はるひめは　いっすんぼうしの
ゆうきに　かんしゃしました。

38

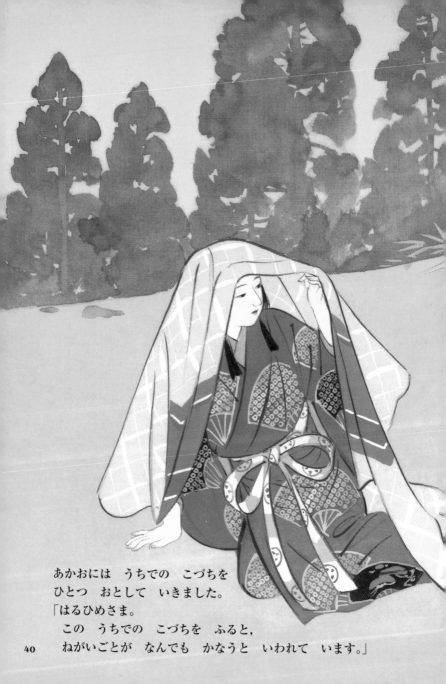

あかおには　うちでの　こづちを
ひとつ　おとして　いきました。
「はるひめさま。
　この　うちでの　こづちを　ふると，
　ねがいごとが　なんでも　かなうと　いわれて　います。」

"But look!" he said. "It left behind
A magic mallet! What a find!
They say that any wish you make
    with one of these is granted!
I read about it in a book."
So Lady Haru knelt and took
The mallet in her hands and shook it
    once or twice and chanted:

はるひめは　おおよろこびで
「ふりだせ　うちだせ　うちでの　こづち。
　いっすんぼうしの　せいを　だせ。」
と，こづちを　ふりました。すると，どうでしょう
いっすんぼうしの　せいは　ぐんぐんと　のびて，
りっぱな　わかものに　なりました。

"May Inchy Bo no more be small!
Brave Inchy Bo, be tall! Be tall!"
And, sure enough, he started
    sprouting up before her eyes.
And so the tiny bodyguard,
By taking heart and working hard,
Was now a hero—*and* a man
    of more than average size.

The Lord of Yojo he became—
A man of wealth and rank and fame—
And in the fall he took
    the lovely Haru for his bride.

やがて　いっすんぼうしは
ほりかわのみやと　よばれる
りっぱな　ぶしに　なり，はるひめを
はなよめに　むかえました。

りっぱな　ぶしに　なった
いっすんぼうしは,
おとうさんと　おかあさんを
むかえに　おおさかに
かえりました。

He brought his bride to Nániwa,
And when his dear old parents saw
Their boy had made his dreams come true,
  they cheered and laughed and cried.

46

And everyone lived happily
Forever after, so, you see,
It doesn't matter if you're small,
Or plump and short, or thin and tall.
It's not the way you *look* at all—
It's what you've got inside.

47

p.7	prayers 祈り　no bigger than your toe 親指ほどの大きさの
	A tiny blessing from above 天からの小さな授かり物　itty-bitty boy ちいちゃな男の子に
p.8	never let that hold him back or get him down それでも彼はしりごみも気落ちもしなかった
	cheerful 元気な　swore 誓った　of great renown 高い名声の
p.11	startled 驚いた　was off to seek his fame 名声を求めて旅だつ　replied 答えた
	as sure as Inchy is my name 一寸法師が私の名前であることが確実であるように
p.12	to get that far そんな遠くに行くには　ought to float 浮かばねばならない
p.13	made a perfect sword りっぱな刀になった　put some food aboard 食べ物を乗せた
	an ear of rice 稲穂を1つ　last her son 息子のいのちをもたせる
p.15	prayed he'd be okay 彼の無事を祈った　as he rowed away 船をこぎながら
p.17	against the current 流れにさからって　all soaking wet ずぶぬれで　far from warm 体が冷
	えきって　nearly sank beneath the waves 波の下に沈みそうになった
p.18	rested in the reeds アシの中で休んだ　valiant deeds 勇敢な行為
P.21	As beautiful as anything he ever dreamed he'd see 見たことがないほど美しく
	rail らんかん　in all its majesty 荘厳に
P.23	all sorts of passersby さまざまな通行人　to and fro 行ったり来たり
	dodged between their feet 足のあいだをひらりひらりと通った
P.25	a huge estate 広大なお屋敷　boldly strode 大胆に進んだ
	wandered through the garden 庭に入りこんだ　loud and clear 大きな声ではきはきと
p.26	His Lordship was amazed to see ～ ～を見て殿はたいへん驚かれた　How now あれあれ
	placed him on his fan 彼を扇に乗せた
p.29	was just his age だいたい同い年だった　And yet それなのに　risked his life 命をかけた
	to save ～ from falling ～が落ちるのを救うために
p.30	far apart 遠く離れて　sigh ため息をつく　If only he were taller! もう少し背が高ければよいのに
	with such amazing speed めざましい速さで　scholar 学者
p.35	female 女性　sneered あざ笑った　reached for ～ ～に手を伸ばした
	screamed and fled 叫んで逃げた　Except for ～ ～を除いて　drew his sword 刀をぬいた
	Touch her and you're dead! 姫に触れたら命はないぞ
p.36	Yum, yum! A snack おいしそうなスナックだ　roared ほえた　swallowed 飲みこんだ
	At least so it seemed そう思えた　that's how it seemed そう思えた
p.37	in the belly of ～ ～のおなかの中で　howled and screamed うなり悲鳴をあげた
p.38	So badly was the monster hurt, 化け物はひどく痛かったので　spit the boy out 一寸法師
	をはきだした　Without you I'd have surely died! あなたがいなければ私はきっと死んでいたわ
	my only real concern 私が一つだけ本当に心配なこと
p.41	A magic mallet 魔法の小づち　What a find! 大した宝物だ　any wish you make with one
	of these is granted これを使って願い事をすると何でもかなう
p.43	May Inchy Bo no more be small! 一寸法師が小さいままでいないように　by taking heart
	and working hard 元気を出して一生けんめいやることで
p.47	it doesn't matter if ～ ～でもかまわない　It's not the way you look at all　大切なのは見か
	けではない　it's what you've got inside 心に何をもっているかである　　　（佐藤公俊）

和英併記 講談社バイリンガル絵本 日本昔ばなし **いっすんぼうし**

1996年 9月27日　第 1 刷発行		電話　03-3944-6493（編集部）
2005年 6月27日　第 9 刷発行		03-3944-6492（営業部・業務部）
		ホームページ　www.kodansha-intl.com
絵	かさまつしろう	印刷・製本所　大日本印刷株式会社
訳 者	ラルフ・マッカーシー	
協 力	講談社児童局	落丁本・乱丁本は購入書店名を明記のうえ、小社業務部宛にお送りください。送料小社負
発行者	畑野文夫	担にてお取替えします。なお、この本についてのお問い合わせは、編集部宛にお願いいた
発行所	講談社インターナショナル株式会社	します。本書の無断複写（コピー）、転載は著作権法の例外を除き、禁じられています。
	〒112-8652 東京都文京区音羽 1-17-14	© 講談社インターナショナル株式会社 1993　Printed in Japan
		ISBN 4-7700-2101-1